This book belongs to:

_____

For Mrs Twirlyhorn and Amazing: Queen of the Forest – F.S.
For Andrea – L.F.

This paperback edition first published in 2022 by Andersen Press Ltd.
First published in Great Britain in 2021 by Andersen Press Ltd.,
20 Vauxhall Bridge Road, London, SW1V 2SA, UK • Vijverlaan 48, 3062 HL Rotterdam, Nederland
Text copyright © Frances Stickley 2021.
Illustration copyright © Lucy Fleming 2021.
The rights of Frances Stickley and Lucy Fleming to be identified as the author and illustrator of this
work have been asserted by them in accordance with the Copyright, Designs and Patents Act, 1988.
All rights reserved. Printed and bound in China.

1   2   3   4   5   6   7   8   9   10

British Library Cataloguing in Publication Data available.
ISBN 978 1 83913 025 0

What Will I Be?

Frances Stickley   Lucy Fleming

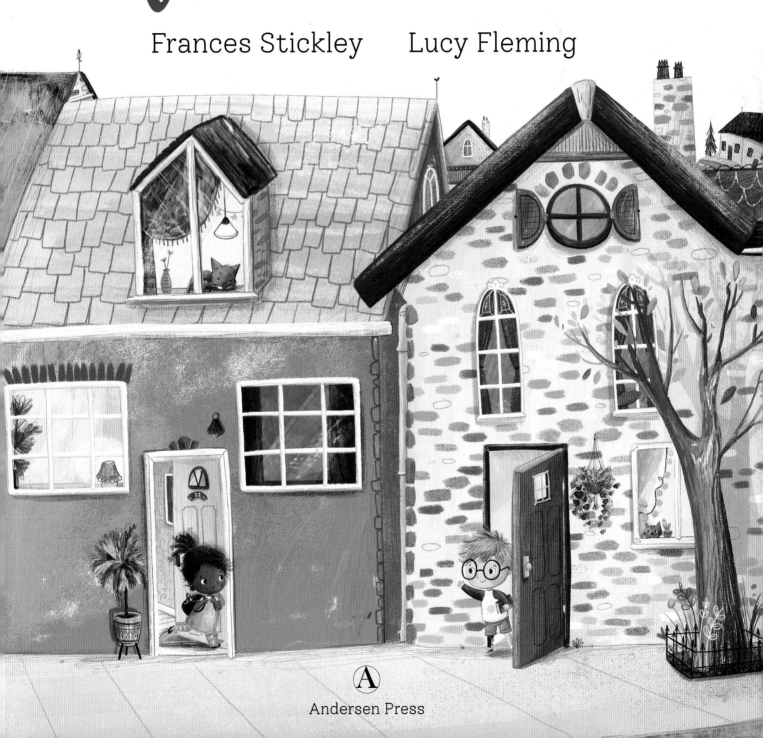

Andersen Press

When you start imagining, there's nothing you can't be.
Will you be a pirate on a quest across the sea,
an engineer with plans and tools inventing flying cars
or blast off like an astronaut and soar among the stars?

Your dreams can be enormous, even though you might be small.
You just need to believe you can be anything at all.

Daddy's shoes are perfect for a silly circus clown. You tiptoe on the tightrope

and you cartwheel upside down.

You take to the trapeze with ease, but... Oooooh! You nearly fall!

Hear the roar!
The crowd wants more!
The greatest show of all!

Then with a whizz, you're Superkids!
The bravest of the bunch!

Here to save the day before
you've even had your lunch!
Leaping through the
living room and
storming up
the stairs,

or battling the baddies with
your trusty team of bears.

Look at all these boxes!
It's a treasure trove in here.
You snip and stick and scribble.
You're inventive engineers!

Robots, cars and dinosaurs –
there's nothing you can't do,
with a great imagination and a
cardboard box or two.

On an expedition as you soar
above the town,
you loop-de-loop in circles and
you zigzag upside down.
Orbiting the planet, then...

Neeeow!

We have a winner!
But can you race the dragons
and be home in time for dinner?

Stop!

It's an emergency!
We need a doctor,
quick!

Rabbit has the
chickenpox

and Daddy's feeling sick!

Don't forget the bandages
and Mummy's magic soap.
Can you hear the heartbeat
with your special stethoscope?

A band of ace-adventurers
explore the forest floor
as you scour the ancient marshlands
on a hunt for dinosaurs!

Now gather up those fossil bones
as quickly as you can.
These could be the greatest finds
since history began!

Look! What's that? A fierce cat!
Prowling through the leaves.
This one calls for Jungle Hero,
swinging through the trees!

Now, creep across the garden…
Sssssh! You mustn't make a sound,

camouflaged and quiet
as you crawl along the ground.

But wait… The sound of footsteps.
It's the mighty King and Queen!
They march you up the stairs
and say, "It's time to get you clean."

But you're the jolly jester and
you try to make Mum laugh,
pulling funny faces as you
climb into the bath.

You're Captain Salty Seahorse
with your crew of pirate ducks.
You're sailing through the soapsuds,
but… Avast, me hearties! Look!

You see the mighty whale winking one enormous eye,
then he flicks you with his tail...

Splash!

You wash up high and dry.

Snug and warm and reading of the places you could go,
when suddenly you're racing
with your huskies through the snow!
You meet a yeti slurping on spaghetti in the ice,
and though she looks quite frightening,
she's really very nice!

You climb into your spaceship,
then you stare out at the stars, and...

Vroom! You're in a rocket on a mission straight to Mars!

The Martians have a party and they ask if you can come, but you zoom back down to Earth because...

"It's time for bed," says Mum.
Come on, brave explorer. Snuggle in and snuggle tight.
It's time to say, 'I love you' as you're turning out the light.

No matter where you've been today –
or when, or why or who,
when you're huddled in a cuddle,
all you need to be is you.

And as you fall asleep,
all the pretending disappears,
then suddenly there's nowhere you
would rather be than… here.

Today has been a whirlwind ride of rockets, capes and wings...
but tomorrow is another day. Who knows what it might bring?

So let your dreams be endless,
even though you're very small.
You just need to believe you can be
anything at all.